Flubby Is Not a Good Pet!

To the kind hearts at the Pat Brody Shelter for Cats—JEM

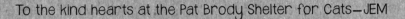

W

PENGUIN WORKSHOP
An Imprint of Penguin Random House LLC, New York

Visit us online at www.penguinrandomhouse.com.

Library of Congress Cataloging-in-Publication Data is available upon request.

ISBN 9781524787769   10 9 8 7 6 5 4 3 2 1

Flubby Is
Not
a Good Pet!

by J. E. Morris

Penguin Workshop

This is Flubby.

He is my pet.

Kim has a pet.

Kim's pet can sing.

The wheels on the bus go . . .

Flubby does not sing.

Sam has a pet.

Sam's pet can catch.

Flubby does not catch.

Jill has a pet.

Jill's pet can jump.

Flubby does not jump.

Run, Flubby!
Run or you will get wet!

Flubby does not run.

No, Flubby! No!

Flubby does not sing.

Flubby does not catch.

Flubby does not jump.

Flubby does not run.

Flubby is NOT a good pet!

But he needs me.

And I need him.